THE STORY OF
A FIERCE BAD RABBIT

THE STORY OF
A FIERCE BAD RABBIT

BY

BEATRIX POTTER

Author of
" The Tale of Peter Rabbit," etc.

FREDERICK WARNE

FREDERICK WARNE

Penguin Books Ltd, Harmondsworth, Middlesex, England
Viking Penguin Inc., 40 West 23rd Street, New York, New York 10010, U.S.A.
Penguin Books Australia Ltd, Ringwood, Victoria, Australia
Penguin Books Canada Limited, 2801 John Street, Markham, Ontario, Canada L3R 1B4
Penguin Books (N.Z.) Ltd, 182–190 Wairau Road, Auckland 10, New Zealand

First published 1906
This impression 1986
Universal Copyright Notice:
Copyright © Frederick Warne & Co., 1906
Copyright in all countries signatory to the Berne Convention

Printed and bound in Great Britain by
William Clowes Limited, Beccles and London

THIS is a fierce bad
Rabbit; look at his
savage whiskers, and his
claws and his turned-up tail.

THIS is a nice gentle
Rabbit. His mother
has given him a carrot.

THE bad Rabbit would
like some carrot.

HE doesn't say "Please."
He takes it !

AND he scratches the good
Rabbit very badly.

THE good Rabbit creeps away, and hides in a hole. It feels sad.

THIS is a man with a
gun.

HE sees something sitting on a bench. He thinks it is a very funny bird!

HE comes creeping up behind the trees.

AND then he shoots—
BANG !

30

THIS is what happens—

BUT this is all he finds on the bench, when he rushes up with his gun.

THE good Rabbit peeps
out of its hole,

AND it sees the bad Rabbit tearing past—without any tail or whiskers!